# THE NURSERY VILLAGE

# MUFFET STORES

*Little Miss Muffet*
*Sat on a tuffet,*
*Eating her curds and whey;*
*There came a big spider,*
*Who sat down beside her*
*And frightened Miss Muffet away.*

COLIN AND MOIRA MACLEAN

KINGFISHER BOOKS

The Muffets kept the village store
Where people shopped each day.

Miss Muffet counted out the change
And helped in every way.

The change was locked inside a till
    Which opened with a key.
One day she went to fetch it, but
    Whatever did she see?

A big round blob with eight long legs
    Was dangling right beside her.
It was the thing she dreaded most –
    A horrid, hairy spider!

Miss Muffet screamed. She dropped the key,
    Which landed with a PLOP!
It splashed into the treacle tub . . .

And splattered all the shop.

The till was locked. Miss Muffet thought,
  Whatever can I do?
The Queen of Hearts has lots of keys –
  I'll borrow one or two.

At last she reached the palace, and
The kind Queen fetched her keys.

"I'm sure you'll get the till unlocked,"
She said, "if you try these."

"Do take this gift," the Queen went on,
    "Of honey in a pot."
Miss Muffet thanked Her Majesty
    And set off at a trot.

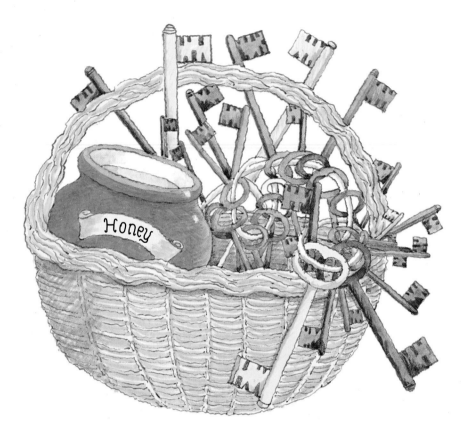

Miss Muffet tried to hurry home
    But what a heavy load!
She took a short cut through the wood
    And strayed far from the road.

Village

BIG DARK WOOD

*Things* creaked and squeaked and flitted past
And all was dark as night.

Miss Muffet hurried through the trees
But then stopped dead in fright.

A Big Bad Wolf was in her path –
He snarled and bared his teeth.

Miss Muffet saw a fallen tree
And dived in underneath.

The Big Bad Wolf came snuffling round.
Miss Muffet crouched and froze.

Then all at once a SPIDER dropped
And wiggled by her nose!

Miss Muffet gave a piercing scream
And, terrified, jumped out.

The wolf was there! She jammed the pot
Of honey on his snout.

And then Miss Muffet heard a shout
Which echoed through the wood.
Her father and some village friends
Ran up to where she stood.

"We searched for you and heard you scream,"
They cried. "Are you all right?"
"Quite safe," she said. "And there's the wolf.
Don't worry, he can't bite."

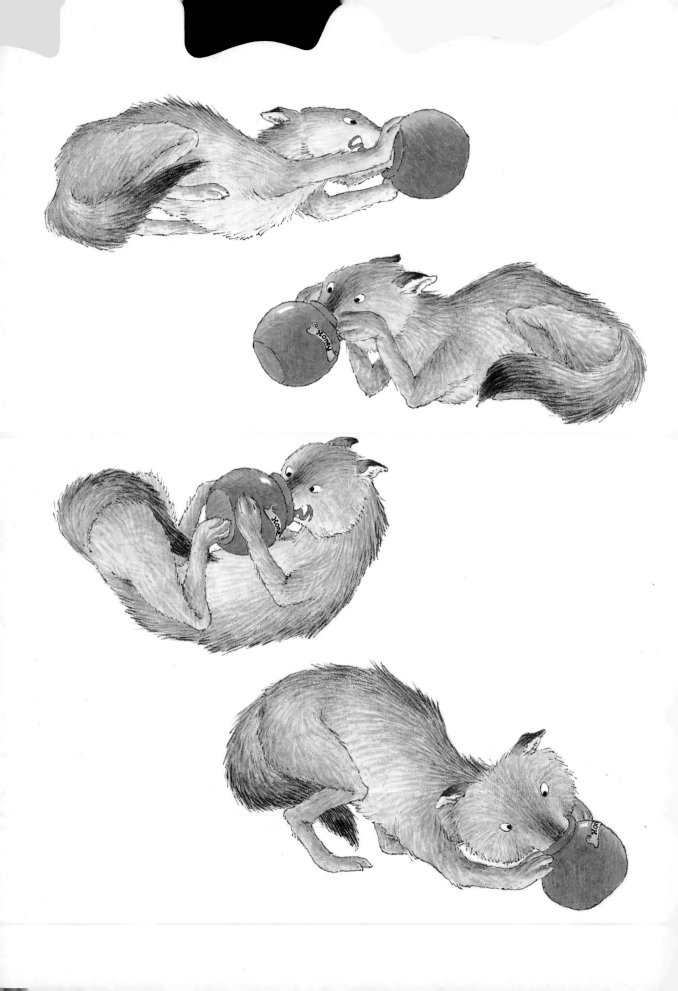

The wolf slunk off. He tried to snarl,
But simply gurgled honey.
Miss Muffet and her friends all laughed –
That wolf looked really funny.

Once back at home, they tried the keys . . .
And tried, and tried, and tried.
The twenty-ninth key turned the lock.
"Hurrah!" Miss Muffet cried.

Miss Muffet's battle with the wolf
Is told until this day.
But we all know that spiders still
Can frighten her away.

# To Vanessa and Camilla

Kingfisher Books, Grisewood & Dempsey Ltd,
Elsley House, 24–30 Great Titchfield Street,
London W1P 7AD

First published in 1990 by Kingfisher Books

BRITISH LIBRARY CATALOGUING IN PUBLICATION DATA
Maclean, Colin, 1930–
    Muffet stores.
    1. Children's stories in English, 1945
    I. Title  II. Maclean, Moira, 1933–  III. Series
823′ .914 J
    ISBN 0 86272 522 4


Phototypeset by Waveney Typesetters, Norwich
Colour separations by Scantrans Pte Ltd, Singapore
Printed in Spain